Stock and Rocket

Published in 2020
by Stock and Rocket, an imprint of
Bonnier Books UK.
Igloo Books Ltd, Cottage Farm, Sywell, NN6 0BJ
www.igloobooks.com

0120 002
2 4 6 8 10 9 7 5 3
ISBN 978-1-78905-841-3

Written by Xanna Chown
Illustrated by Jacqueline East

Cover designed by Bethany Dowling
Interiors designed by Justine Ablett
Edited by Stephanie Moss

Printed and manufactured in China

This book belongs to:

....

Stock and **Rocket**

Time for Bed

It was bedtime, but Pip Panda was wide awake.

"Can I have one more story?" he begged Dad. "Pleeeeease?"

Dad laughed. "Okay, Pip," he said. "Just one more."

He opened up Pip's storybook and started to read.

Pip enjoyed the story, but he still wasn't sleepy.
"Your night lights will help you feel cosy and dozy,"
said Dad. He switched on the **twinkly** lights above
Pip's bed and said goodnight.

Dad was just settling down in his armchair, when he heard a noise coming from the kitchen. He found Pip, filling up his beaker with water from the fridge. **"I'm a little bit thirsty,"** explained Pip.

Dad tucked Pip back into bed again, but he hopped out.
"I left my blanket in the kitchen," he explained.
"I'll get it," said Dad. When he returned, Pip was
rummaging through the wardrobe.

"Now what are you doing?" asked Dad.
He quickly ducked, as a woolly jumper **flew** past his ear.
"My feet are cold and I can't find my warm socks," said Pip.
Dad helped Pip find his socks, then he said goodnight again.

"Wait!" said Pip.
"I need something to cuddle!"
He **jumped** up and started to search his
room, checking every nook and cranny for the
right toy. At last, he found Big Ted, stuffed
down the side of the cupboard.

Dad said his third goodnight, and started
to leave, but Pip yelped, **"Don't go!"**
"What do you need now?" sighed Dad.
He was beginning to feel a bit tired himself.
"Can I have a goodnight kiss?" asked Pip.

"Of course," said Dad, kissing Pip on the head.
"Is there anything else you want before you go to sleep?"
But this time, Pip didn't answer. He was so tired from
getting in and out of bed, he was already asleep!

Camping Fun

Sunshine Forest was the perfect place to camp. Chrissie Crocodile and her friends **tumbled** out of the car, excitedly, ready for adventure.

"I can't wait for tonight," shouted Chrissie.

"Me too," said Mia Monkey.

"Me three," said Erin Elephant.

"What's so special about tonight?" asked Mum, who was putting up the tent.
"That's when we're having our midnight feast," said Chrissie.
She couldn't wait to stay up late, toasting
gooey marshmallows on the campfire.

Dad asked the girls to collect wood for the fire, so they **dashed** off into the trees, picking up twigs and **dragging** branches back to the tent. "Good work," said Dad. "Now you can go and play."

First, they **raced** to the rope swing and took turns **soaring** through the air.

Then, they found a stream and got soaking wet as they paddled in it, slopping **gloopy** mud into a pile to make a tiny waterfall.

After their picnic lunch, Dad organised a sports challenge. Mum cheered when Chrissie came first in the running race.

Mia was the best at tree-climbing and Erin's long trunk helped her win the water fight, too. **SPLISH-SPLASH!**

Mum hung their wet clothes up to dry and the girls changed
into their PJs, ready for a delicious tea of sausages and beans.
While they ate, Dad told **spooky** stories, which
made them **scream** and **giggle**.

As it got dark, the girls snuggled up next
to each other beside the campfire, in their warm
sleeping bags. **"I'm tired,"** sighed Mia.
"Me too," said Erin, yawning.
"Me three," said Chrissie. **"Can we have our
midnight feast tomorrow, instead?"**

"Of course!" said Mum. "The fresh air and exercise must have tired you out." "How about just one marshmallow before bed?" asked Dad, but the girls were already asleep, so he popped one into his mouth. "Ah well, there's always tomorrow."